Kids lo[...]
Choose Your [...]

"When I figured o[...]
the back, I al[...]"

Sophia DeSento, age 9

"I read them because they are
interesting, and they have lots of cool
titles and words to use."

Laini Ribera, age 9

"There can be at least 28 ENDINGS
in it and so many choices. Other books
you have to read the whole book in
order, well not this one!"

August Backman, age 10

"I like that you can choose.
So, if you want to choose something,
you can do it."

Colin Lawrence, age 10

"The CYOA books are crazy because
there so many crazy choices."

Isaiah Sparkes, age 12

SPIES: JAMES ARMISTEAD LAFAYETTE

BY KYANDREIA JONES

ILLUSTRATED BY GABHOR UTOMO

CHOOSECO®
WAITSFIELD, VERMONT

Choose Your Own Adventure Spies: James Armistead Lafayette
© 2019, Chooseco LLC,
Waitsfield Vermont. All Rights Reserved.

Illustrated by: Gabhor Utomo
Book design: Stacey Boyd, Big Eyedea Visual Design

For information regarding permission, write to:

CHOOSECO

P.O. Box 46
Waitsfield, Vermont 05673
www.cyoa.com

Published simultaneously in the United States and Canada

Printed in Canada

10 9 8 7 6 5 4 3 2 1

To Kale K who always has my back.
And to Jane who taught me to constantly
ask What If?

Lastly, to Gabriela "Gib Gab" Brissett
the reader of all my stories.

BEWARE and WARNING!

This book is different from other books.
YOU and you alone are in charge of what
happens in this story.

Your name is James Armistead Lafayette. You
began life as an enslaved person on a plantation
in Virginia. But with the help of a young French
general, the Marquis de Lafayette, that is about
to change.

General Lafayette is fighting on the side of the
young leader George Washington and asks YOU
to become a spy for the Revolution. It can lead to
freedom! When you read this book, you will learn
real things about what life was like for you in the
1780s. You will also make choices that determine
YOUR own fate in the story. Choose carefully
because the wrong choice could end in disaster—
even death. But don't despair. At any time, YOU
can go back and make another choice, and alter
the path of your fate...and maybe even history.

The smoke is what wakes you. You sit up on the dirt floor of the quarters where you sleep. You cough as you breathe more smoke. Your eyes sting.

"Fire!" someone yells from outside. You suddenly hear wood beginning to crackle. The fire is close. You can see the orange flames through a wide crack between the wallboards. Quickly you stand up.

"Wake! Now! Everyone!" you yell to the sleeping figures crammed into the small room.

But the people sleeping on rough mats around you barely stir after their backbreaking day in the tobacco fields. Some moan in response. You grab the young twins who are asleep next to you, Edgar and Eliza, and head out the door.

This time you bellow as loud as you can. "FIRE!"

Turn to the next page.

2

It is the middle of the night. The smallest cabin is aflame. But how? People stumble from the shacks nearby. Your friend Frederick yells, "Water!" and runs toward the blaze with a bucket.

Your good friend Miranda helps form a line from the creek behind the nearest tobacco barn. "Water," she yells. "We need water!"

Others join her, passing buckets of water hand to hand.

The year is 1781 and you are an enslaved person named James Armistead. You live on a plantation in Virginia. You run to put the two small children on the other side of the clearing where they will be safe. Just as you set them down, you see the brush at the edge of the woods rustle. A tall head ducks and disappears into the thicket.

Go on to the next page.

It is a head you would recognize anywhere. It belongs to your childhood friend John. You couldn't help but notice the small sack of belongings slung over his shoulder. It means one thing: John is trying to escape.

Did he start the fire as a diversion? Is there anyone else with him? And what will their escape cost the others they leave behind? you think wearily.

Edgar suddenly screams and points at the inferno.

"Mama!"

He's right. His mother, Elizabeth, sleeps in the quarters that are on fire. The twins have been sleeping with Miranda, her sister, ever since her husband and her older daughter were sold last month. Elizabeth has not been well since they left.

Without another thought, you cover your mouth with the tail of your shirt and run toward the burning house.

Turn to the next page.

4

Before you can reach the door, a voice calls to you. "James!" It is Elizabeth. She's safe! And she hands you a bucket of water, pushing you to the front of the assembly line where your strength can be put to use. You were built for this moment.

The muscles in your arms forget their aching as you douse the flames bucket by bucket. You cannot lose hope. You must stop the fire from spreading to other buildings.

You take another bucket, climbing onto a log. You continue to throw the liquid onto the burning roof. Commotion from the plantation's main gate startles you. You crash to the ground, the bucket in your hand smacking you in the head as you go.

Everything goes black.

Turn to page 7.

You awaken several hours later. Soot and ash coat your body. Your head hurts, but you are awake. You are alive.

A cloth forms the shape of a triangle overhead, secured by pegs and ropes. You are inside a tent, alongside other victims of last night's blaze.

As you get up and step out into the sun, a well-dressed young man approaches you, turning a document in his hands.

The man wears a striking blue overcoat with gold embroidered around the collar and pale cotton breeches. A white cloth puffs out from his neck in crisp ruffles. The black hat under his arm catches your attention: the broad rim, and three red, white, and blue feathers. You have never seen anything like it.

Turn to the next page.

8

You read the words on the document, smiling as you do: VOLUNTEER ENLISTMENT.

The man extends his hand in greeting. You take it nervously, and then he surprises you by saying your name: "A pleasure to meet you, James Armistead." He has an accent. He shakes your hand.

"I am General Marquis de Lafayette."

You lower your eyes modestly. A general! You cannot believe it. You are shaking hands with a member of the Revolutionary Army, and he knows who you are.

Before you can recover from your surprise, General Lafayette continues, "I have heard what you did for your people last night. My men and I saw the flames from town and rode here to help. If it was not for your courage and your bravery, many lives would have been lost in the fire."

You are quiet, focusing on the general's words of praise. General Lafayette lays his hat beside you. "Please, sit. I have a proposal for you."

General Lafayette gestures toward the plantation. "Here, on this farm, as you know, you are not a person. You are hands for picking crops. You are arms for carrying supplies. You are legs for dancing to someone else's tune. All this you are, but a person you are not."

Go on to the next page.

"For your bravery," General Lafayette says, "I will help you reach freedom. The army for the revolution needs help. If you want to fight alongside me, I have brought enlistment papers from the state of Virginia. Your master has already signed them. However," he adds, lowering his voice. "If you want to claim your freedom by yourself, and do not wish to join the revolutionary forces, I will keep your secret."

You are stunned by General Lafayette's kindness. Your temple throbs where the bucket hit your head. General Lafayette looks at you, waiting for your answer.

If you decide to join the Revolutionary Army, turn to page 10.

If you decide to find freedom on your own terms, turn to page 16.

10

You take the enlistment papers from General Lafayette. You scan the document, scribbling your signature on the dotted line. You feel the general's eyes on you. You glance up to see he is watching you with a bewildered expression.

"You can read!" he says, surprised.

"And write," you add. These are the first words you utter to the general. This time it is you who extends a hand. "Honored to meet you, sir," you say.

Master Armistead, your owner, walks up to the two of you. He notices the signed document in General Lafayette's hands. "Well then," he sighs, clapping a steady hand on your shoulder. "It appears that your country needs you, James. We will have to find a way to carry on without you."

Turning to Master Armistead, General Lafayette puts on his hat. "We lost a day's journey, tending to your fire," the general says, removing Master Armistead's hand from your shoulder. "We must push on. The revolution awaits."

General Lafayette gives you a uniform before exiting. You dress quickly and step out of the tent, aware of the gaze of the enslaved people who remain here. You nod to them. They return the gesture. You translate their smiles as encouragement.

Go on to the next page.

Humming to yourself, you shuffle to join the other soldiers. The careful drum of conversation ceases upon your presence, magnifying your steady melody. The soldiers take notice of you, halting the music on your lips.

At first, they are silent and then the plantation shakes with their laughter:
HAHAHAHAHAHAHAHAHAHAHAHAHAHAHA!

You bow your head. Where did the general go? Your face burns with embarrassment. You feel a hand on your arm. You look up to see your friend Elizabeth, smiling and offering you a cloth.

"They are laughing at the ash," Elizabeth says.

"Thank you," you say, cleaning the residue from your skin. "Did you hear the news?"

Elizabeth nods.

"Good for you, James. A soldier! Good luck."

Your excitement returns, "I am going to fight in the revolution!"

Turn to the next page.

12

One of the soldiers approaches. You brace yourself for the worst. Too much of your blood has been spilled by the hands of white men. You flinch as the soldier lifts a leather strap. It could have easily been struck upon your back. But this isn't a hostile conversation. He hands you the strap gently, and you take it.

"The name is William," he says. His face breaks into a lopsided grin. There is something in his eyes. Curiosity? Mischief?

Go on to the next page.

"Sir?" you ask, raising an eyebrow. You are careful to address him with respect, even though he seems friendly. Your uniform may match his, but he remains white and you remain black. Yes, you have won your freedom. However, equality is another battle altogether.

"William," he insists, correcting you. "You are one of us now!"

You smile in appreciation, but you notice William doesn't shake your hand or take a step toward you. He points to the strap he's just given you.

Turn to the next page.

"That bridle is for Liberty," William says, gesturing to the lone black horse beside the others. Your mouth drops at the sight of the magnificent beast. Its legs are full of power. Its black mane glistens. You cannot hide your excitement. You have never ridden a horse before!

"Liberty," you repeat, stroking the reins in your hands.

Two more soldiers walk up, flanking William. They are expressionless. The general is nowhere in sight.

"Do you want to learn to ride?" William asks, prompting snickers from your growing audience. "Or would you rather pull our carriages yourself?"

You clench and unclench your fists. Surely, he is baiting you.

If you decide not to engage in William's tricks and look for the general, turn to page 24.

If you head toward Liberty the horse, turn to page 67.

Master Armistead believes you have joined the Revolutionary Army. In truth, General Lafayette covered your tracks so you could escape slavery. You are deep in the forest east of your plantation.

Freedom is yours for as long as your feet can carry you. You considered the risks: slave-catchers, wild animals, starvation. The enlistment papers in your coat offer some protection. The knife in your pants pocket offers a bit more. You also have a week's worth of food in the bag Elizabeth prepared for you. You can hunt small game when that runs out. As for the wild animals, you hope nothing too big finds you out here alone in the woods.

You know exactly what to do with your freedom. You are on a mission to find John and the other fire starters. You are not sure what you will do when you find them. You grew up with John. The two of you used to play in the fields together. You loved to see who could run the fastest.

John always won until he twisted his ankle, running errands for Master Armistead. That ankle never healed right. Speaking of that ankle, you are sure the drag marks in the dirt are John's. You are about to follow them when you hear a strange crunching noise.

*If you investigate the noise,
turn to page 18.*

If you follow the marks, turn to page 127.

18

You glance up at the bright, full moon. You travel at night for safety, but it's difficult to see and you don't dare carry a lit torch. You can hear everything. The *whoo whoo's* of the owls. The sound of insects chirping in the night. A mosquito lands on your neck. You slap it dead, wiping the smashed bug on your breeches. You hear the noise again. It sounds like something eating.

Crunch crunch crunch.

This time you are sure that it's right behind you. You do not dare to breathe.

Go on to the next page.

Your own voice surprises you as you appeal to the unseen foe. "D-d-d-d-o not." Your words rattle in your mouth. You clear your throat and try again. "Do not come any closer."

You take out the knife from your pocket. If needed, you will use it to defend yourself.

Turn to the next page.

20

You walk toward the crunching noise carefully, one foot in front of the other. Carefully, you bend down and push back the leaves on the bush in front of you. At first, you do not see anything. Then, you feel warmth on your forehead and see two furry legs in front of you. Your lips quiver as you raise your eyes to face the animal. You nearly fall over from laughter at what you see. It is only a dog!

"Hello," you whisper to the animal. It is a small dog, a puppy. Probably less than a year old. The puppy yips, licking its chops. It sniffs your shirt. "Yes, hello, little buddy," you say to the dog. You feel the presence of someone behind you.

Turn to page 22.

"Hello," a small voice says, startling the puppy. You turn to see a child no older than Edgar. He wears well-made but worn clothing. From the looks of it, he spends a lot of time scavenging in fruit bushes or escaping the jaws of the forest's tiny beasts. You look past him, wondering if there was anyone else with him. All you see are shadows. He seems to be alone.

"Do you need help?" you ask him.

"Yes," he says. "Hello, little buddy," he says, in a soft, high voice, leaning down to the puppy. You give him an odd look. He's repeating what you've said.

Something does not feel right. You hear more crunching. It seems to come from all around you. The child gestures for you to follow him. Your instincts tell you to make a break for it, but it is clear that the child needs your help. What are you going to do?

If you trust your instincts and run, turn to page 27.

If you choose to follow the child, turn to page 34.

You find General Lafayette standing beside a trellis draped in grape vines behind Master Armistead's house, whispering to someone out of sight. His back is to you as you approach quietly. You only catch bits and pieces of the general's conversation:

"You are a genius," General Lafayette says. "They will never suspect...victory is ours...so long as...and the best part is...It will be glorious!"

Who is he talking to? You crouch down, concealing yourself to avoid suspicion.

"Now if only we can..." the general continues, "do you think...but what if we...We will need someone brave and resourceful and strong to..."

The general is hatching a secret plan! The scraps of information intrigue you. Are these battle plans? Does the general talk to himself as a means of strategy? And what happened to his hair? His head is shiny and bald.

Go on to the next page.

The general continues talking, "Washington is going to…I can smell their blood now…this country shall be…"

Washington? Blood? You are anxious. Maybe you should stop eavesdropping and return to the other soldiers.

You cannot remain in a crouch for much longer. Your knees ache. You shift your weight, snapping a twig under your leg. You cower back as the general whips around.

"Who is there?" he asks. His voice is much higher than it was earlier. "Show yourself!"

Leaves crunch as the general makes his way to your hiding spot. He is nearly upon you.

If you confront the general, turn to page 42.

If you flee the scene, turn to page 48.

26

You help the general, successfully defusing the situation. The Pamunkey want exactly what you and everyone who fights wants: what is best for their people. You do not speak the Pamunkeys' language but you understand their gestures. The pain in their eyes. Their pleading hands. The bullet hole in one of their children.

"Medic!" you call, sending for the doctor. The man does what he can for the young boy. After the child is treated and seems better, the Pamunkey leave you and your squadron to continue your journey.

"James," says General Lafayette. "How did you do that?"

"I see them as I myself want to be seen," you say. "I do not immediately assume that they wish to bring me harm. I study and then I act based on my observations."

"That is good thinking, James," says the general. He considers this point, nodding to himself. "Very good thinking indeed."

Turn to page 61.

You run, darting deeper into the forest. The crunching noise is deafening now, coming from all directions. You ignore it, stumbling your way through the dark. The moon's light barely shines through the branches.

Your skin prickles with unease. The child's voice remains in your ears, mimicking your greeting to the dog, "Hello, little buddy."

Suddenly you hear it all around you, high-pitched and terrifying: *Hello, little buddy! Hello, little buddy! Hello, little buddy!*

Your heart beats in your ears. You see a touch of scarlet a little way in front of you. You would normally avoid approaching a camp, but now you dare to take a chance. It could be John or other slaves on the run. The odds are slim but anything is better than the sounds tormenting you.

Turn to page 29.

You approach the scarlet fire, and realize you've made a terrible mistake. It is a camp full of slave-catchers. There is a symphony of low growls. Your eyes settle on the dark forms next to the fire. A pack of bloodhounds rise beside the flames. Drool drips from their mouths. You make eye contact with one who licks its chops in response.

You stand in place for what feels like ages. Your ears suffer the frantic beatings of your heart. *BOOM BOOMPH. BOOM BOOMPH. BOOM BOOMPH. BOOM BOOMPH.*

As if hearing your pleading heart, the dogs let out a vicious snarl. Instinct pushes you a step back. This is a mistake. The beasts bark one after the other. Men and women step out from the tents. It is too late to move.

"You!" a woman shouts. "How did you get away from the others?"

The day's excitement proves too much. You faint in response to the women's question.

Turn to the next page.

30

You awaken in shackles. You raise the chains to your face in horror. When you put your hands back down, they graze the shackled hands of people on either side of you. The weary brown faces of men and women meet your tired eyes.

"Where are we?" you ask them quietly, swallowing back your urge to cry out. The man chained to you shakes his head. The woman presses a finger to her lips. She runs that same finger across her throat. Then, she shushes you again, though her gestures have already stunned you to silence.

You quickly recover, finding your voice. "Please," you say. "You have to help me. I do not belong here. I must...I have..."

Where is your bag? All your belongings are gone. Thankfully, you tucked your free papers into your trousers. Your papers! Phew! You have papers! You chuckle in triumph.

HEHEHEHEHEHEHEHEHEHEHEHEHE
HEHEHEHEHEHEHEHEHEHEHEHEHEHE!

"Stop," the captured slaves snap in unison, but you cannot help yourself. Your laughter only increases.

"Is there something funny?" a voice questions.

Turn to page 33.

"That is because they are different from you and me. They have their own culture, dialect, and rules," says Andrew.

"Not to mention they are downright savages," adds Matthew.

That is a word you recognize. "They probably can say the same of us," you say.

"What was that?" asks Matthew, barely listening. He is absolutely mesmerized by the Pamunkey. "Look at those spears!"

"Perhaps to them," you say, a little louder, "*we* are the savages.*"

"We are not the ones who have odd rituals and who walk around without much clothes," counters Matthew, suddenly offended.

"But you are the ones who treat your fellow men worse than livestock," you say.

A scream prevents you from saying more. You dismount Liberty.

"You better leave the negotiations to the general," says Andrew. "Our history with them is not the best."

If you go help the general, turn to page 26.

If you follow Andrew's advice, turn to page 103.

A tall red-haired woman stands in front of you. She holds a whip in her hand. Two other women stand on either side of her. The red-haired woman wears a uniform similar to the soldiers back at the plantation, but faded and stained with red blood. You answer her question with a croak, "No, ma'am."

"I'd like a laugh myself," she says. She looks at her companions. "We love to laugh, right ladies?"

The women answer her with a hearty cackle.

The red-haired woman crouches down where she stands. You are close enough to see the brown in her eyes. They are the color of the dark black clouds that rose from the plantation fire. She asks again in a voice that cuts like glass, "What is so funny?"

If you distract her with a song, turn to page 41.

If you tell her the truth, turn to page 51.

34

As you follow the child, you notice familiar drag marks under the moonlight. The child is leading you to John! You let out a sigh of relief. You smile when you reach a small yellow house, not questioning its place so far from civilization.

There do not seem to be any enslaved people on this farm. You do not see lodging for them nor any fields that would require their hands. What do the people who live here do? How do they live out on the edges of the woods? Who owns these lands?

The child leads you to a red barn adjacent to the yellow house. When he opens the big barn doors, you are shocked by what you see. A crowd of people stare at you but you do not pay them any mind. It is the woman standing at the front of the room who captures your attention. It is Elizabeth! She does not greet you nor does she seem happy to see you.

"Sam," Elizabeth says, addressing the child who brought you, "what have you done?"

Sam points at you, sticking a skinny finger into your thigh. "Chosen one," he says. "Fated."

Turn to page 37.

Rise and shine.
Welcome your son
Up before the sun.
Rise and shine.
Oh, Mama, quit your mournin'.
Rise and shine.
I'll see you in the mornin'.
Rise, rise, rise,
and shine
Like the sun, up before your son.

Mama, quit your mournin'.
Oh, rise.
Yes, rise.
Come on and rise
like your son.
Shine. Shine. Shine.
Like the morning sun.

"Beautiful indeed," says the red-haired woman, dabbing at her eyes with a handkerchief. Enchanted by your singing, she pulls a key out of her pocket. You hold out your wrists. Your companions do the same. One by one, you are all unchained. You keep singing, clapping your freed hands together. You sing as your brothers and sisters in bondage scatter into the forest.

The End

"What is going on?" you ask, speaking to Elizabeth only. You pepper her ears with questions. "What is all this? How did you leave the plantation? Where are Edgar and Eliza? Who are all these people?"

"We are the Secret Organization established to help you win America its independence," Elizabeth says.

"Me?" you say. "What do you mean?"

"James, you were born to be a hero," she says. "You are compassionate and daring and you put the safety of others above your own."

"But what does that have to do with all this?" you ask, gesturing toward the crowded barn.

A booming voice speaks behind you, halting Elizabeth's response.

"James," John says. "You are a bit ahead of schedule."

Turn to the next page.

"Your country needs you," says John. You do not respond. You have no idea what is going on. All you remember is the fire. The bodies. The smell of burnt flesh is still ripe in your nostrils. You raise an eyebrow at John.

"And you were needed—to start that fire? Causing people we cared about to burn to death so *you* could escape? I'm certain the people who helped you are among us now."

You scan the room for the other fire-starters.

"They are not here," says John, reading your mind, "and the fire was not as bad as you think."

"At least seven people perished in those flames," you say, bewildered by his remarks. "Men, women, children."

"Are you certain that they are dead?" asks John. A grin settles on his lips.

"Am I certain?" you huff. "I carried them all out myself. Their bodies difficult to hold due to the Reaper's heavy hand!"

"Surely, the bodies felt heavier and heavier as you picked one up after another?" asks John. "Perhaps, your fatigue played a role in that weightiness?"

"What are you saying?" you ask him. "I know what I saw."

Go on to the next page.

John gestures to the long table on the left. Seven people stand from their seats: two women, two men, and three children. You recognize their faces from the pile of bodies. It cannot be! The dead have risen! You suddenly feel sick. You clap a hand over your mouth, forcing yourself to swallow back vomit.

"What if I told you," asks Elizabeth, "that the fire was only a test?"

"A test?" you echo. "A test...for me?"

"Yes," says John, "we had to be sure that you would risk your life for your people."

"When you did," continues Elizabeth, "we steered General Lafayette toward you."

"He was so surprised by your valiance that he offered you a chance to serve in the Revolutionary Army!" adds John. "But you declined his offer."

"Initially, we were angry and confused," says Elizabeth, "but then we figured that your journey in the woods would give us more time to prepare."

"Prepare for what?" you ask. This question animates everyone in the room. They all respond in one voice: "War."

Turn to the next page.

40

"War with whom?" you ask, staring back into the unmoving faces.

"Those who keep us from freedom," says John.

"What do we know of freedom?" you mutter, tightening your fists. Elizabeth and John exchange glances.

"We know that it awaits us," they both respond.

"Now that Sam has brought you here," says John, "you must find Lafayette and join his army."

It was Sam who led you here, showing you the truth. He also made some strange comments to you along the way. Maybe there are other things Sam knows that John isn't telling you? Though John and Elizabeth may have misled you in their "test," it would be an honor to fight among such heroes and to help bring glory to this land. Yet, you are aware of the risks. Bullets, cannonballs, knives, and other enemy soldiers could easily claim your life out there on the battlefield. What future awaits a former slave like you?

_____

If you agree to go back and fight alongside Lafayette, turn to page 58.

If you decide to ask Sam some questions first, turn to page 62.

If you do not trust John or Elizabeth and choose to decline their offer, turn to page 66.

"There is nothing funny about this," you confess, buying yourself time. "But I do remember a song I used to sing when I was young."

"You better not waste my time," says the red-haired woman. The women on either side of her give their two cents:

"Time is precious you see," says one.

"The jewel of our existence," says the other.

"Back in the fields," you say, drawing from your experience on the Armistead Plantation, "the other slaves and I would sing this song to help the work go along faster. My friend John learned it from a man he met on the road once. It is a rather beautiful song, I think."

"Go on," commands the red-haired woman, giving you room at last. You are happy that she no longer looms over you. "Sing it for us."

Turn to page 56.

"James," says General Lafayette as you step out from your hiding spot. "How much of that did you hear?"

"Eh…" you say, trailing off. His baldness surprises you, but even more surprising is a tiny squirrel, nestled in the general's fancy wig. General Lafayette places the tiny creature directly onto his freckled scalp before returning the wig to his head. Your eyes go wide. Not only does Lafayette keep a squirrel under his wig, he tells the squirrel his plans for battle!

Go on to the next page.

"I am sorry, sir," you say, finding your voice. "You disappeared and I was wondering where it was you could have gone and…"

"That is enough, James," says General Lafayette, holding up a hand. "It is quite all right."

"It is, sir?" you ask, exhaling. Being a soldier is different from being a slave. Being caught spying and listening would have gotten you whipped hours ago.

"Well," sighs General Lafayette. "I imagine that you got an earful."

"I could not hear too well," you say. "Just bits and pieces."

Turn to the next page.

"Chestnut and I have big plans," says General Lafayette, patting his wig.

"Chestnut?" you repeat.

"I am referring to the squirrel in my headpiece, of course," says General Lafayette.

"It is none of my business what a man keeps in his wig," you say. You are happy that the squirrel is not a figment of your imagination.

"It very well may be," says the general. He clears his throat, parking himself on the grass. He pats the ground beside him. You sit.

"Humans can be so cruel," sighs General Lafayette. "They put chains on one another, beat, cheat, whip, burn, kill each other...

"But squirrels," he says as Chestnut peeks from its hiding place. "They are truly remarkable creatures. They are all about survival. Did you know that they hoard food and hide it in up to a thousand places?"

"No, sir, I did not know that about squirrels," you say, scratching your head. A laugh flutters on your lips.

General Lafayette continues, "Well they do. Squirrels are important to this revolution! They are born naked and toothless and blind. Can you imagine that? Being so vulnerable and defenseless?"

"What do squirrels have to do with the revolution?" you ask finally, surprised at his seriousness.

Go on to the next page.

"The squirrels are a metaphor," answers the general. "Imagine, James, that *freedom,* the concept of freedom, is nuts, berries, and tree bark. Like squirrels, we human beings have hoarded and scattered bits and pieces of liberty in every nook and cranny of this land. We all know where these buried treasures lie. Their scents are fresh in our nostrils. Liberation is a matter of retrieving these treasures before the other squirrels...I mean... other *people* stuff their cheeks with our glory, our honor, our destinies."

You lower your eyes. *Your* concept of freedom is very different today than it was just days before, when you were a slave on this very plantation. You wonder what your future will hold, and where General Lafayette will lead you.

"Does everyone have a claim to these treasures or are they allocated for a limited few?" you ask finally.

"That is the purpose of a revolution, James. We *all* have hope that life will change. Nothing is promised. If you want freedom, you have to fight for it. Hope is perhaps the only light in battle and it is one that burns brighter with each success. So, too, it grows dimmer with each lost soldier."

Turn to the next page.

46

"Is that what you meant about the blood?" you ask, recalling the general's conversation with Chestnut.

"Do not tell me that you are suddenly squeamish," he teases, smiling a small smile. "Are you not the one who ran toward the inferno?"

"It is not that," you say quickly. "I have seen a lot of blood spilled in my life."

"Right," says the general. "You have had your fair share of tragedy. But does that not make you all the more inspired? You have much more to gain than you have to lose."

"What about my life?" you counter. "Surely, I have yet to lose that."

"Look around," answers the general. Your fellow enslaved people have resumed working, having already lost a morning of labor. The soldiers talk among themselves, waiting for their general to return. "This is not a life."

"Going from battle to battle is all well and good," continues the general, "but we have not yet won until something better awaits us on the other side of this long war."

"Does Washington offer us something better?" you ask.

Go on to the next page.

"*General* George Washington is the most important name you will ever utter," says General Lafayette. "You are very much like the land in which you live, James. Young, chained, struggling to be taken seriously. You will like Washington. Should you meet him."

"I am sure you are right, sir," you say, rocking on your heels. "But what were you saying about victory? About needing someone smart and brave and resourceful and strong?"

"I do not believe that I said 'smart,'" he points out. "Soldiers do not need to be very intelligent, *per se*. They only need to go where glory thrives. Spies, on the other hand…"

Chestnut runs up the general's arm. Its little paws tickle his neck. The man chuckles. You do not think that you can keep your laughter at bay anymore. Though some of the general's strange ramblings inspire you, the squirrel makes the whole situation ridiculous…You know neither what to believe nor how to react. Is the general the revolution's champion or a madman with a squirrel?

"Perhaps I have said too much," says the general, watching the complex emotions of humor, confusion, and wonder play upon your face. "You look at me as though I am a fool, James. Do you think I am a fool?"

*If you say no, and urge him to continue,
turn to page 75.*

*If you finally let out your laugh,
turn to page 82.*

You leave the general and fall in line with the other soldiers, marching east until nightfall. General Lafayette stops you all to make camp for the night. You grab equipment to pitch a tent. When you are finished, you head into your shelter to sleep. William's shadow appears in the entrance.

"What do you think you're doing?" asks William.

"Can I help you, William?" you sigh. It has not yet been a day since the two of you met and you already tire of him.

"Thank you for pitching me a tent," says William. "It is nice to see that you remember your place around here."

"I thought that you said I was one of you now," you respond, fighting a yawn. It is so difficult to tell if William is teasing you, or actually being cruel. Maybe he does not know himself.

"So General Lafayette claims," says William. "He says that he sees something in you. If I were you, I would start convincing people that he is right."

"Do you always question your general's instincts?" you ask. The words surprise you. As do the ease at which they leave your mouth.

Turn to page 50.

50

"Watch yourself," says William, clenching his jaw.

"I always do," you respond, unmoving. He makes a beeline for your tent. You step in front of him.

"I suggest you move," says William. Again, you feel the watchful eyes of the other soldiers. This time you do not feel as moved to let the insults go.

If you have had enough of William, turn to page 85.

If you decide to let it go and repay William later, turn to page 88.

"Ma'am," you begin, deciding to tell her the truth. "I am not what you think I am."

"No?" muses the red-haired woman. "What are you then?"

"I am a free person," you say before launching into the story about the fire and about General Lafayette's reward.

"You were freed by a general you say?" she says, nodding intently as she listens to your grand tale of freedom.

"Let me see those papers," she says, finally, thrusting her hand out for them.

"Would you please release me so that I may retrieve my papers?" you ask, glancing down at your shackles. You speak with as much politeness as you possibly can. The last thing you need is for her to feel threatened by you or angered by your fortune.

"Do you take me for a fool?" she huffs. The women on either side of her chime in:

"Yeah, do you think you are smarter than her?" inquires one woman.

"Do you think you can take the three of us and these dogs if you are freed?" asks the other.

Turn to the next page.

52

"No, ma'am," you say, being sure to lower your eyes. "There is no other way."

"Do not try anything," warns the red-haired woman, removing a key from her pocket.

"You will regret it if you do," says one woman, letting out another cackle.

"There are worse things than shackles," agrees the other.

"That is enough, clucking hens," snaps the red-haired woman. She turns to you, releasing you from your chains.

"Ah," you say as the weight falls from your wrists.

"Go on now," the three women say. The act unsettles you but you are giddy with joy as your hands enclose your papers.

"Ah ha!" you say, pulling them out in triumph. "See! I am free!"

The three women huddle around you, taking the papers from your grasp. They study the documents carefully, flipping through the pages and following the words with a finger.

Go on to the next page.

"Well," says one woman.

"That sure is something," says the other.

You peek at the pages held in each of their hands: they are all upside down.

"We cannot read," confesses the red-haired woman.

"I can," you say. "It says that I am free."

"It could say anything," says one woman.

"That is correct," agrees the other. "For all we know this is all one big ruse. Some far-fetched scheme."

"I swear it," you say. "I am free!"

Turn to the next page.

54

"No," says the red-haired woman, ripping up the pages. "You *were* free."

"No," you argue, watching the woman throw the pieces into the fire.

"Stop," you say, falling to your knees.

"You cannot be this discouraged over some ripped paper," says one woman, as her red-haired friend swallows the remnants of your freedom.

"Truly," says the other woman. "We have yet to release the dogs."

The End

You clear your throat, obeying with your song:

> *Mama, quit your mournin'.*
> *I'll see you in the mornin'.*
> *Rise and shine! I'll see you soon.*
> *But if I should meet my doom,*
> *well, Mama, I'll see you then too.*
> *I'll come back home to you.*

The more you sing, the more engrossed the women become. They sway to the music, rocking to your melody. The enslaved people at your sides also summon the courage to let the words part from their lips. This encourages you. You continue:

So Mama, quit your mournin'.
I'll see you in the mornin'.
I'll make it to the mornin'.
I'll make it to the mornin'.

The women join you in voices that cause birds to flee from their branches. You do not mind it. You sing louder, letting your voice's power lift you from the ground. So too, all the others rise beside you.

Turn to page 36.

58

General Lafayette welcomes you back with open arms. You are accepted into the fold by your fellow soldiers and given a horse named Liberty. During your journey, the carriages make a sudden stop. There is commotion at the front of the charge.

"What is going on?" you ask, watching General Lafayette confront a group of people that look like no one you have ever seen. They wear the most beautiful clothes, vibrant with reds, yellows, oranges, and greens. All of them have their hair down to their shoulders. Some keep the strands in long, elaborate braids.

"Wow," you say. You are in awe despite being yards away.

"That is the Pamunkey Tribe," answers one of your comrades, Matthew. "They are the most powerful tribe in Virginia."

"Tribe?" you repeat, unsure what the word means.

"Yes, tribe," answers another comrade, Andrew. He goes on to explain, "A tribe is a group that shares familial, social, economic, and religious practices as well as a common way of life."

"They do not look like either of us," you say.

Turn to page 31.

"Sir?" you say.

"James," he says, walking you back to Liberty. "There is a man that I want you to meet."

You have earned General Lafayette's respect. He is impressed by how well you use your ability to empathize with others as a means of understanding their arguments and their motivations. He introduces you to General George Washington, who vows to put your talents of negotiating conflicts toward triumphing over the British.

The End

"Give me a moment to think," you say to John and Elizabeth, rubbing your temple. You are tired. It's been a very difficult twenty-four hours! You turn to look for Sam and see he's standing beside you still, looking up at you.

"Chosen," says Sam. His perfect posture and unwavering stare prickle your skin. You have the sudden feeling he's not a child at all, but a small, old person. You meet his gaze.

"I'd like to speak with Sam," you say carefully. "Alone."

"Are you sure, James?" asks John, exchanging a glance with Elizabeth.

"Sam is just a child," says Elizabeth.

"He seems like the person in charge here," you insist, sticking to your decision.

"I am," says Sam as clear as day. He snaps his fingers. The statue-people stand, marching out of the barn.

Go on to the next page.

"Sam is not what he seems," whispers Elizabeth before leaving. "Proceed with caution."

Sam sits in the middle of the room. You remain standing, watching as the young boy closes his eyes and clasps his hands together.

"Errrr," you say. "Sam?"

"Chosen," Sam chokes out, opening his eyes. The hazel irises glow. "James Armistead Lafayette."

"Lafayette?" you say. "I am James Armistead."

"Only in the present," responds Sam. "What is important is not who you are now, but who you will be."

"Who I will be?" you ask. "How could you possibly know that?"

The room trembles as the child speaks in a voice without youth, his words like marble:

> *The freedom that you seek*
> *will be yours if you wish to take a peek,*
> *I can show you what I see:*
> *a road that leads directly to liberty.*

Turn to the next page.

64

"What road?" you ask. "Sam, please, I do not understand your rhymes."

He ignores you, continuing his prophecy:

This road is full of struggle and pain
from which you stand to gain.
Though, you must be weary
of the decisions you make
some paths you choose will be a mistake
and your life, body or soul
they are sure to take.

"I am not scared," you say to yourself. You are thankful when Sam closes his eyes again. His hazel irises unnerve you.

"I am not scared," you repeat, clutching one of the chairs.

"Sometimes you will need to be," says Sam.

Go on to the next page.

*Sometimes you will need to be afraid as
fear will keep you on your toes.
When you reach the bloody path,
take the thorns with the rose.
Walk through darkness
until you find the light.
Know when to stray from battle
and when to fight.*

"Sam, enough rhymes," you say. "Sam?"
The child does not seem to hear you, continuously repeating his first set of rhymes:

*The freedom that you seek
will be yours if you wish to take a peek,
I can show you what I see:
a road that leads directly to liberty.*

"You want to show me what you see?" you ask, listening to the words at last.
"Chosen," says Sam, nodding. "Fated. James Armistead Lafayette." He reaches out his hands to you, palms up.
You are not sure if you can trust Sam. Elizabeth did warn you to be careful.

*If you allow Sam to show you your future,
turn to page 124.*

*If you rather try your luck with John and
Elizabeth after all, turn to page 128.*

66

"How am I supposed to trust any of you?" you ask. "This is too wild! Me? A fated hero? This is my first day free from slavery and you're asking me to risk my life?"

"James…" starts John.

"I am done putting out your fires," you say, shaking your head. "Lest I receive more than a bump on the head the next time."

"Think about our future," says Elizabeth. "Surely, that will make all the risks worth it."

"This is the first time in my whole life where I can say that I belong to myself alone," you say. "I will not cheapen this body by putting it through someone else's war."

"Chosen?" says Sam, looking up at you.

"I have made my decision," you answer, preparing your belongings to leave. "I am now the master of my own destiny."

The End

How hard can it be? you think, standing beside your new horse, Liberty. She is much larger than you expected up close, stretching a foot above your head. You reach out to touch her face. She blows out of her nose, startling you.

"Whoa," you say, leaping back.

"Are you sure you do not want any help?" asks William, watching from a safe distance. The other soldiers have left his side, and he seems friendlier. But you can't be sure. And you feel you must prove yourself.

"I don't need any help," you say, keeping your eyes on Liberty. "She and I are just getting acquainted is all."

"Looks like you could use some guidance," insists William, tapping his foot. "We would like to set off before sunset if it's all the same to you."

"General Lafayette is unaccounted for," you respond. "So I have time. That is unless you plan to leave without your general?"

William huffs, crossing his arms. You return to Liberty, trying to calm her by acting calm and confident yourself.

Turn to the next page.

"Hello, Liberty," you say, speaking softly to the horse. "My name is James."

"James it is then," says William as you reach a hand out to pet Liberty's nose. She lets you pet her, blowing happily all the while.

"Atta girl," you say, placing the saddle on her back and looping the bridle and reins around her head. Even if you haven't ridden a horse, you know how to do this. "Those boys over there will not bother you any. It is just you and I."

Go on to the next page.

You mount Liberty, taking the reins. Everyone has stopped to look at you. You give William a look of triumph. He clicks his teeth in response.

"Squeeze her with your legs to get her going," he tells you.

You follow his instructions, squeezing your legs together and thrusting your weight forward. Liberty moves.

"She is moving," you say. "I am doing it! Whoo hooo, Liberty! She is moving!"

You do the motion again, urging her to go faster.

"Go slow, James," warns William, but Liberty has already increased her trot, dashing forward. You hold on to the reins for dear life.

Turn to the next page.

"James!" cries William, running after you. "Stop her! Stop her! Stop her!"

The other soldiers watch as you and your horse ride frantically around the plantation. You miss the house and the carriages by the skin of your teeth. Pulling the reins this way and that. All the while Liberty races:

CLIP CLOP CLIP CLOP CLIP CLOP CLIP CLOP CLIP CLOP CLIP CLOP CLIP CLOP

"I do not know how to stop," you say, using all the strength in your back and legs to remain on the horse.

"Pull the reins backward," says William, diving away as Liberty nearly tramples him. He looks ahead of you, worry in his eyes. The other soldiers are paying attention now, and they leap out of her path.

"Pull the reins backward!" shout your fellow soldiers. All around you, everyone seems to scream the same phrase: "Pull the reins backward!"

You close your fingers around the thick ropes in your hands and squeeze backward. Liberty comes to a halt, hurling you over her head. You land on something that breaks your fall.

Turn to page 72.

"Ouch," a voice says. There is a red, white, and blue feathered cap beside you. You landed on General Lafayette! You quickly get up, helping the general stand. William and the others rush to the general's aid.

"Sir, are you injured?" asks William, rushing to help.

"I am sorry, sir," you say, beginning to apologize profusely. "I do not know how she got away from me. I understand if you—"

"You may both unhand me," says General Lafayette. "I am quite all right."

"I did not mean to cause you any harm, sir," you insist as the general dusts himself off.

"Not to worry, James," he says, shaking his head. "We all remember our first time on a horse."

"Sir, how is he supposed to join us in the war," starts William, "if he cannot ride into battle?"

"It seems like he was doing fine until it was a matter of *stopping* the animal," says General Lafayette to William. "And I know that you, being my best rider, will help James ride as well as any of us."

Go on to the next page.

"But, sir," William begins to argue but then shakes his head and thinks better of it. He does not want to challenge his commanding officer. "It will be my pleasure, sir."

"I do not doubt it," says General Lafayette, putting his cap on and limping over to his own stallion.

"Just my luck," mutters William once the general is out of earshot.

"Thank you for telling me how to stop," you say.

"I very well could not have you crushing the good general, could I?" responds William, picking up Liberty's reins.

"I suppose not," you say, looking down at your boots.

"Come along, James," calls William. "You heard the general. We have work to do."

You take your place beside William as you and the troops march out of the plantation.

Turn to the next page.

Although the relationship starts off rocky, you and William become great friends as a result of your lessons. You two fight side by side in battle, protecting and serving General Lafayette above and beyond your call of duty.

Your continued bravery and willingness to defend those closest to you improve your rapport with the other soldiers. They accept you as one of their own. You never shy from death with them by your side. You lead them through the dark when the somber shadows of war befall you. Your past has taught you to survive all that threatens to crush your body, mind, and will to fight. You pass the drive to surmount hardship on to your general, on to your comrades, and on to the birth of your new country.

The End

"I do not think that you are a fool," you say to General Lafayette, sucking your laughter back in. "Please continue, sir."

"Very well then," he says, settling into the discussion. "James, do you know where I am from?"

"A place called France," you say. You remember reading the word on your agreement. It did not mean much to you.

"Yes, very good, James," says General Lafayette. "I come from a beautiful country 4,760 miles away from here. I have traveled all the way across the North Atlantic Ocean by ship, to aid in the revolution against the British Empire."

"That seems like a long way to get involved in someone else's war, sir," you say.

"It is a long way," agrees General Lafayette. "I suppose that I could have very well kept to myself, but you are mistaken when you say that this revolution is not mine. It very much is. The French and British have been rivals for some time now. We have suffered too many defeats from them."

"You are here for revenge?" you ask.

Turn to the next page.

"Revenge would be good," says General Lafayette. "However, ensuring that the colonists escape Britain's tyranny would make victory all the more sweet. A new country? Oh, the thought of it makes me smile! So many possibilities and opportunities! *That* is what I fight for as much as I fight to win glory in the name of my people."

"Is it hard?" you ask. "Coming here and speaking a new language? Leading people who are not your own?"

"Although this land and my own have had our differences," says General Lafayette, petting Chestnut, "forgiveness and understanding go a long way during conflict."

"I suppose they do," you agree.

"James," says General Lafayette after a while, "I think I am in the middle of hatching a very daring operation. It seems that you are the person that Chestnut and I have been looking for! You are brave and strong and resourceful."

"What were you thinking, sir?" you ask.

Go on to the next page.

"We have intel that there is a British camp not too far from this plantation," says General Lafayette. "How would you like to infiltrate it?"

"Infiltrate?" you repeat. You do not know what the word means.

"You could sneak into the camp," muses General Lafayette, tossing the squirrel happily in the air. "You can pose as another cook or a stable hand or a slave!"

"You want me to go back to being a slave?" you ask.

"Oh, heavens no!" says General Lafayette, unable to contain his excitement. "I want you to pretend so that no one guesses what you are really doing. What you will really be is a covert spy, gaining information that could help us win the war!"

"Sir, slow down," you say, having trouble following the general. "You want me to walk into their camp and win a revolution that you have long been fighting?"

"You will have to disguise yourself, of course, and keep your true identity a secret," answers the general. "But who says that one person cannot win this war?"

Turn to the next page.

"It does not take a telescope to see an army coming," adds General Lafayette, "but no one is ever looking for a single person. James, cannot you see, it is you who will lead us to victory?"

"I can see it, sir," you say, standing taller.

"Yes!" celebrates General Lafayette. "There's the James who pulled his people from the fire!"

"Where do we begin?" you ask.

If you decide to infiltrate the British camp right after the general's motivational speech, go on to the next page.

If you choose to infiltrate the camp disguised as a medic's assistant, turn to page 111.

If you decide to spy on the camp posing as a slave, turn to page 116.

After the general's powerful speech, you decide to infiltrate the British army as a spy.

You ride your horse, Liberty, into a city known as Richmond, ablaze with fire. You and Liberty pass by destroyed houses, the mills in shambles and the factories burning. The devastation is so complete that you know these fires were an act of war.

Turn to the next page.

80

You and Liberty find remnants of a British camp near what once was a saloon. You are surprised to see a tiny tent abandoned but still standing. You inspect it, sifting through reams and reams of blank pages. *These are an odd thing to have,* you think. *Must be why the troops did not take these with them.* A noise startles you. You watch a squirrel run across the tent's entrance. You jump back, spilling a full carton of ink.

"Oh no," you say as the dark liquid spreads onto a pile of the blank pages. You pick up the sheets, noticing words forming everywhere the ink grazes. The liquid is too thick to read anything. You run your hand across the page, smearing black onto your palms. You see triangles, arrows, and wavy lines. Rivers. You turn the paper clockwise. Something in this drawing reminds you of the ride you and Liberty just took.

This is a battle plan.

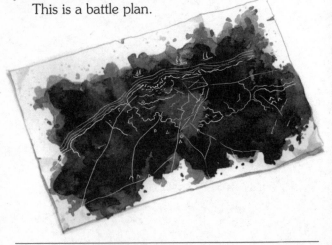

Go on to the next page.

You spread the papers out, using your stained hands to reveal a map of a place called Yorktown. One of the pages has words written on it. You read them out loud: "We are sending our troops to Yorktown. We will need more men as the town is unfortified and vulnerable. Send reinforcements as soon as possible. The war depends on it."

"I can't believe it," you say.

You have done it! You have found a key piece of information to end the war! General Lafayette is going to be so proud of you!

The End

You cannot help yourself. You slap your knee, chuckling. A squirrel leading a revolution! You fall backward from laughing so hard. A shadow looms over your bent frame. You make *eye* contact with Chestnut.

"Do you think that I am joking?" asks General Lafayette.

"I think that you are a bit mad, sir," you say, wiping tears from your eyes.

"Let us ask the others, shall we?" he asks, heading toward his awaiting troops.

"I do not know if you should do that," you say.

"This is the only way to convince you," he insists, standing on a box. Everyone quiets to hear the general's announcement. Chestnut remains on his shoulder, busying itself with a treasure it has found in the general's wig.

"Attention, *mes amis,*" says General Lafayette. You stand away from him not sure what to make of the current events. "Tell me, do you all see this animal resting so sweetly on my shoulder?"

Go on to the next page.

"Of course," says one voice in the crowd. "That is our dear old Chestnut," replies another.

"Grandson of my late Cashew," says yet another voice. "May she rest in that great oak tree in the sky."

You cannot believe your ears. What are they all going on about? Is it not strange to house an animal in one's headpiece? Especially that of such a high-commanding officer in the Revolutionary Army?

"Errrr," you say, interrupting the long appraisal of the late Grandma Cashew. "Is no one the least bit concerned about this animal?"

"Why would we be?" asks William, standing out from the mass of men. "We all have one. None of which compare, to Chestnut, of course. That is no surprise, as he is a legacy."

"You all have one?" you repeat. Your question prompts every soldier to take off their wig. You are stunned to silence by the sheer amount of small mammals produced on top of each head. You pat your own thick hair, inspecting the tight curls as if you too have unknowingly been a part of this harebrained scheme.

Turn to the next page.

84

"James looks sick," William says, eyeing you with his usual smirk. His squirrel seems to smirk as well. You blink, hoping it is all a trick of the eyes.

"Dear James," says General Lafayette. "You must not be so quick to dismiss the extraordinary as impossible or terrifying."

General Lafayette offers you Chestnut. Not knowing what else to do, you hold the creature.

"Instead of laughing in the face of those different from yourself," continues General Lafayette as Chestnut runs along your shoulder blade, "intelligent people must constantly ask questions and be receptive to even the very unusual answers."

Only one question seems important to you: how hard did that bucket hit you on the head?

The End

"No," you say. You're done with William!

"What did you say to me?" asks William.

"I said no," you say, a little louder. You stare back into his eyes, unwavering.

"Odd," says William, using a finger to clean out an ear. "I keep mishearing you. It sounds like you are refusing a direct order."

"You are neither my general nor my master," you say. "You have no right to order me around or to treat me as if I am beneath you."

"You have been wearing my uniform for less than a day and suddenly you are my equal?" mocks William.

"I was born your equal," you reply. "Now we both know it. Dislike me as you might, even you will have to honor that."

Turn to the next page.

"James is right," says General Lafayette, startling you, William, and the onlookers. He must have heard your discussion from his tent.

"Sir," says William, saluting the general. "It is only that…"

"Enough," says the general, holding up a hand. "Let this be the last time I hear any of you treating James this way. In my troop, we do not engage in this type of foolishness. What is it that we are fighting for? Honor? Liberty? Respect? Do you believe these words turn to air in James' ears?"

"Sir, no, sir," respond the soldiers in unison. William is sure that his voice is heard above the rest.

"Have you all forgotten that we are struggling for independence?" asks General Lafayette. "Is this not ironic as we condemn those like James to rest in chains? In my troop, we recognize this injustice and we fight for James' freedom as much as our own. That is the condition of the agreement that James and I hold. Now, who among you dares to make me a liar?"

"Not I, sir," all the men say one by one.

"Not I, sir," you say as General Lafayette turns to you.

"Not, I, sir," says General Lafayette, returning your salute. "At ease."

The End

"James," says William, catching you. He throws your arm around his shoulder, running for cover.

The soldiers around you shoot at the invisible enemy without so much of a sound to confirm or deny their victories. One by one, they all fall to the ground. So too, your mouth fills with blood. The arrow has pierced your chest.

"James, why on earth would you…" starts William. He is unable to finish his inquiry, stunned by your act.

"Save Lafayette," you gasp. These are the last words you will ever speak as you die in William's arms.

The End

You park yourself near the bonfire, frustrated by your own decision to let William boot you from your tent. All the other soldiers have turned in for the night, leaving you to sharpen your knife by the blaze. Though you are upset about what happened between you and William, you are thankful for the heat on your skin.

"Who does William think he is, anyway?" you grunt. "I am as much of a person as he is!"

You hear a rustle in the night. A man steps up to the fire and out of the pine trees surrounding it. He inches toward you. His eyes settle on the leftover soup, in a cauldron over the fire.

From his ragged clothing and bare feet, you gather that he is a runaway slave. He points a finger at the soup, asking you for it with his eyes. Neither of you want to disrupt the safe silence that covers the campground.

Turn to the next page.

90

Your hand reaches for the soup but you pause. If you are caught helping the runaway, your loyalties will be questioned. William will have enough leverage to make General Lafayette reconsider his decision to enlist you.

General Lafayette has shown you kindness. But he granted you your freedom: this man is probably still considered someone else's property. Helping him is a crime, and you have a responsibility as a soldier.

You could wake the others so the decision is not yours alone to make, but you fear they would pick the very worst. They could even kill this man for trying to escape.

Perhaps if you take the man down yourself, you will have more control of his fate? There is a risk that he will overpower you. Though he has missed a few meals, he is tall and young. You remember the slaves who set the fire to escape. They were powered by something very strong to cause all of that damage and take all of that risk.

You press a finger to your lips, a signal to keep quiet, while you think. The man nods at you, his eyes scanning the camp.

---

*If you decide to fight and capture him,
go on to the next page.*

*If you decide to wake the others,
turn to page 93.*

If you give him the soup, turn to page 97.

You decide that it is better to intervene in this man's fate yourself. Your life may depend on it.

You pick up the soup, pretending that you will hand it to him. When he reaches for the meal, you make your move. As soon as you lunge at him, you know that you have made a mistake. Your soup spills over the two of you as you both topple onto the ground.

The man pushes you with all his force. You fall backward, striking your head on a log in the exact same spot on which the bucket had fallen. The young man abruptly disappears from your view. You slip into the black.

Turn to the next page.

92

"James! James!" someone calls, leading you out of unconsciousness. You open your eyes to the sight of a man you don't recognize holding a cap with red, white, and blue feathers on top of it.

You stare at this strange man in front of you, rubbing your aching head. You can't remember how you got here, to this campsite in a pine forest.

"James," he says again, looking at you with a troubled expression.

"Ow," you groan, looking from side to side and then behind you.

"You have been out for ages, James," says the man.

"Who is James?" you ask finally.

"My dear friend," he says, "you are."

The End

You don't want to risk this man's life, but you also don't want to risk your own. Maybe if you alert the others but do nothing, he can get a head start escaping.

"Intruder!" you yell, waking the others. "Come quick!"

As soon as the words leave your mouth, the runaway man turns around and races back into the forest. Your fellow soldiers quickly take up arms and head toward you. "Where?" asks William, followed close behind by a growing party. "Which way?"

You point your finger in the opposite direction that the man had gone. Led by William, the search party heads off on a fruitless mission.

Turn to the next page.

94

A tall stranger approaches you back at the bonfire, accompanied by General Lafayette. He stretches to at least six feet. He is not as tall as your friend John, but he is very close. Even under the dark cover of night, you take note of the man's powerful stature and commanding presence. You also realize how small the general looks in comparison.

"What is all the commotion?" asks the newcomer.

"There was an intruder at the camp, sir," you answer. "Are you George Washington?" you guess.

"How did you know that?" asks General Lafayette.

Turn to page 96.

"In *this* country, many people know my name," answers General Washington. "I am a very important man."

"How could I forget," says General Lafayette in a joking voice. "It has been but ten seconds since you last told me."

General Washington ignores his friend's remark, correcting your earlier comment, "It's *General* George Washington."

"Yes, Sir, *General* George Washington."

"Very good! It is of the utmost importance that the people around you address you properly, my new friend eh…"

"James Armistead."

"Ah, but of course. Marquis has been talking my ear off about you," says General George Washington, gesturing to General Lafayette. "Speaking of which, he and I have an idea. I must admit it is a tad *moonstruck*—you know, *odd*."

You are barely listening, having noticed General Washington's teeth. They are very discolored, and do not seem to quite fit his mouth. They look like they hurt him. He catches you staring, but he does not look offended. He and Lafayette look jolly instead.

If you decide to discuss the generals' moonstruck idea, turn to page 118.

If you choose to ask General George Washington about his teeth, turn to page 120.

You pick up an empty tin from beside the fire and dip it into the heavy soup pot for the stranger. He pulls the tin from your grasp, nodding his thank you before gulping down the meal. You hear a rustling noise, louder than any sound one man could make. You and the stranger both freeze with anticipation. The rustling stops.

"Deer," you guess.

"Bigger," says the man, setting the tin down. You hold out your knife and pull another from your boot. "And very close."

"If I was you I would run," whispers the man. "Run," he repeats, following his own advice and disappearing into the bushes.

There is movement in the corner of your eye. You turn, slashing at the air. William's hand stops your frantic movements. He sucks his teeth as blood runs down his forearm.

"What is the matter with you?" he asks, snatching the knife from your grasp. He reads the fear on your face, drawing his gun. You may not like each other but you do recognize that danger takes precedence over your rivalry.

Turn to the next page.

98

"Something is watching us," says William, returning your knife to you. He presses his back to yours, staring at the forest. One of the trees moves.

"John," you say, exhaling the breath you had been holding. You have celebrated prematurely. The giant of a man falls forward, an arrow sticking out of his back.

"It is a Pamunkey!" says William. "The most powerful tribe in Virginia."

Pa-whatie? You do not have time to question William, moving to help your fallen friend.

"John!" you shout, rushing to his side.

Turn to page 100.

100

William rushes into the night, waking the others with his gunfire. Soldiers run from their tents. Many are met quickly with an arrow to the skull. You watch a man drop from the trees without regard for the bullets being shot at him. He raises his bow, pointing it at William.

Without thinking, you jump in front of William as the man releases the arrow.

"Ooff," you grunt, staggering. You have been hit!

Turn to page 87.

You follow your comrade Andrew's advice, leaving the negotiations to General Lafayette.

You and the army head toward Rappahannock River, where a friend of General Lafayette awaits. You reach a white small house in a town called Fredericksville, Virginia. A man stands outside, resting on the wooden fence with an air of composure and dignity. He wears a large white wig clasped in a ponytail and a blue uniform embroidered with golden thread. Although he stands at nearly six feet tall, he appears to shrink as the soldiers surround him. He holds his blue cap in his hands, fiddling with it as he speaks.

"My beloved Ferry Farm will not be where we rest our bones tonight," jokes the man, earning chuckles throughout the ranks. "I have no idea how my parents, three brothers, my sister, and I made do. These days, I am afraid that this charming pile of wood only houses my treasured copies of Shakespeare."

"Worry not," says General Lafayette. "We will make do. There is someone that I would like you to meet."

You stand wide-mouthed behind the general. Andrew nudges you. "I believe that that someone is you," he says.

Turn to the next page.

104

You dismount Liberty, throwing the reins to Andrew. You straighten your hat before you present yourself to the two men.

"This is our newest recruit, James," says General Lafayette. "James, this is the General George Washington."

"Nice to meet you, James," replies General Washington, releasing his grip on his cap to give you a quick, firm handshake. The general lowers his voice as he turns his attention to General Lafayette, asking, "Shall we discuss business inside?"

"*Oui, mon ami,*" answers General Lafayette, commanding his men to set up camp with a wave of his finger. You start back toward your horse, Liberty, but General Lafayette stops you. "James will be joining us."

General Washington does not argue, retreating into his modest childhood home. You follow General Lafayette inside.

"Please, sit with us," says General Washington, gesturing toward the small wooden table. You and General Lafayette sit, waiting as General Washington brings tea.

Go on to the next page.

105

"Marquis, did you receive my letter?" General Washington asks General Lafayette, blowing steam from his cup.

"Why do you think I brought James here?" responds General Lafayette. General Washington spits out his tea. He takes a moment to collect himself, dabbing at his mouth with a handkerchief.

"You cannot be serious," he objects. "Do you have any idea how important this is?

"Why would you like to put the fate of my country in James' hands?"

General Lafayette shares your heroic story, following it with the fact that you found him after days apart all on your own. You do not correct him. Who would believe that you had the help of two escaped slaves and a magical child? You have a hard time believing it yourself.

"I must say that is an incredible story indeed," admits General Washington once General Lafayette finishes. "James, you are a hero in the ranks of Juliet or Hamlet."

Turn to the next page.

106

"James," says General Lafayette. "We are discussing your future. You surely have a say in it."

"Whatever you need, sir," you say. "I can do it."

"We need you to spy on the British for us," says General Washington, cutting to the chase. "We need you to go into enemy territory, gather useful information, and get it back to us. Preferably without dying or getting caught."

You hear Sam's voice in your head. *Chosen one. Fated.* Would accepting this position mean you are betraying your friends? Are you truly destined to save your country?

"Look what you did," says General Lafayette. "You have startled the poor kid."

If you decide to spy for the Revolutionary Army, go on to the next page.

If you decide your loyalty lies with the Secret Organization, turn to page 123.

107

"I am not scared," you say. "I will be a spy for the Revolutionary Army."

"I knew it!" cheers General Lafayette, standing in triumph. "I have found our champion!"

"Settle down," shushes General Washington. He uses his handkerchief to clean up the spilled tea as he and General Lafayette begin to talk war strategies.

Turn to the next page.

108

The next morning, you set off on foot to find the British army general Lord Charles Cornwallis. You leave your horse, Liberty, behind. It is easier to navigate the Virginia terrain alone. You also abandon your Revolutionary Army uniform. You dress in simple clothes so that you may enter the British camp without being noticed.

You head east, discovering the British Army in the Chesapeake where the water is sparkling, wild and blue. You are surprised by the amount of black men you see among the ranks. The soldiers seem more preoccupied with preparing for war than with your sudden appearance.

Go on to the next page.

You find General Lord Cornwallis standing alone, holding a folded letter in his hands as he looks out into the Chesapeake Bay.

You squat down, staying out of the general's eyesight. He talks to the letter, his voice breaking as he speaks:

"Dearest Jemima, we are headed to Yorktown. It is not the best location...the Yankees could find us and we'd have no place to go but the ocean."

"Oh Jemima," he continues, "this war has been long. Yorktown may be my only chance to return home to our children victorious. I suppose there is my answer. To Yorktown we shall go!"

Spying is easier than you think! You tiptoe away from the heartbroken man, carrying his secret back to the generals. It is this secret that wins you and America independence—and you even get to keep your horse, Liberty, too. Despite your successes, you have also made enemies in the Secret Organization who believe that you left their cause for your own glory. You always sleep with one eye open as you fear that one day Sam will pay you a visit.

The End

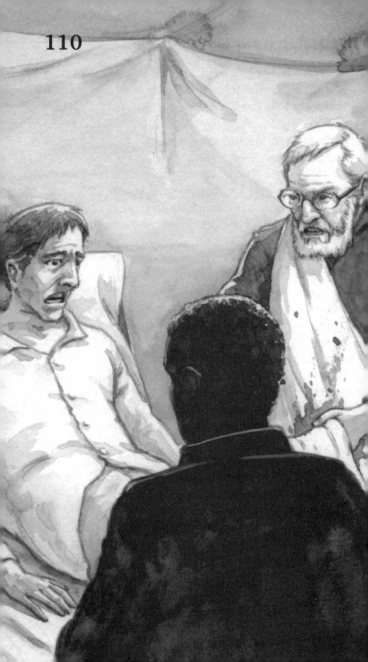

After strategizing with General Lafayette, you infiltrate the British camp under the cover of the medic's assistant. You accompany Dr. Baker everywhere. You keep close to the wounded because they are the most likely to talk. You think this will be easy, but it is very hard to ask questions when the patients are being treated for sickness and war injuries. You learn that those on the brink of death always have a word or two to say.

"This is no revolution, it is war," says a soldier, peering down at where his leg used to be. He does not say how this injury happened. "It is a bloody and cruel and agonizing war."

"Mind your mouth, soldier," says Dr. Baker, looking through his thin spectacles. "You are a soldier for the British army, lad. Pray you act like one."

"My leg!" answers the soldier, not daring to touch what is left of his limb. You cannot help but stare. "I am no longer a soldier without it!"

"Were you left behind on the battlefield?" asks Dr. Baker, changing the wound's dressing.

"No," winces the soldier. "But what good am I if I cannot walk?"

Turn to the next page.

112

"Your tongue seems fine," says the doctor. "Perhaps it will lead you to places that your legs never could."

With that, the doctor leaves you alone with the soldier. You look down at him on his cot. His injury is horrible, maybe you should let him rest. He shivers and you rise to get him a blanket. The wounded soldier grabs your arm, halting you.

"Please," he says. "Stay with me."

Go on to the next page.

"It is worse than losing a leg," says the soldier as you sit beside him. "It is feeling it. I wake up and I forget sometimes that it is no longer there."

"I offer my sympathies," you say. "But it is true that you have a voice in what happens next. Maybe you should say something about what you're seeing on the battlefield."

"You wager that I sing the Revolutionary Army into submission?" he jokes.

"No," you laugh. "I do not think General Lord Cornwallis would fancy that."

"Ha! That man is a bit of a fool," he admits, coughing.

"What do you mean?" you ask.

"I should mind my mouth," he says, coughing a bit harder. "I should not have said that. I do not know what has come over me."

"It is only us," you say.

"Well," he says. Beads of sweat make a necklace around his neck. You should probably call for the doctor. "The general plans on going to Yorktown."

Turn to the next page.

114

"What is Yorktown?" you inquire, wiping sweat from the soldier's face.

"Please," he says. "Get the doc. I am feeling ill."

"One moment," you insist. "What is Yorktown?"

"Ah!!!" cries the soldier, reaching for his injured leg.

"What are you doing?" you ask, quickly holding his hands.

"It hurts!" he yells. "It really hurts!"

Go on to the next page.

Dr. Baker returns upon the soldier's cries. "This is not good," he says, reassessing the wound. "Not good at all."

"What is it?" you ask.

"It is worse than I thought," he answers.

You both watch as the soldier struggles in bed. He is never able to tell you what he meant by Yorktown, succumbing to his wound. He gave you a lead. You need only pull the thread. Just like that the plan of Yorktown unravels. You use the cipher book to send the news to General Lafayette and his good friend General Washington.

You write:

237,	Gentlemen,
625 72 683	The British will
220 632 Yorktown.	go to Yorktown.
591 635.	Send troops.
682 683 249 224.	We will have glory.
— 708 188, F.	—your friend, J.

To the amusement of future generations and historians, you send this important message by carrier squirrel.

The End

Lafayette and Washington talk you through a plan and you carefully examine a map together, but you must complete this mission entirely on your own, including the long journey there. You leave everything, including your military uniform, behind you, and infiltrate the British camp wearing the clothes you wore the day you met Lafayette. The British camp is large. No one ever thinks much of you. One day, a bit of chitchat about the revolution catches your attention. You hide out of sight, listening to the conversation.

"How long do you think this war is going to last?" asks the food hand, Gumbo.

"Hopefully not another eight years," replies Tap, a recruit from Charlottesville. "I am not as young as I used to be."

Edison, the youngest of the bunch, arises his eyes to the trees. "I hear the Revolutionary Army uses squirrels to eavesdrop on enemy soldiers," he says.

"You heard what?" asks Gumbo as Tap says, "What type of foolishness?"

"Think about it, there are always squirrels around here," says Edison. "What do you think that they are doing?"

"Being squirrels!" says Tap. "We are in the wilderness. This is where they live!"

Go on to the next page.

"Squirrels cannot talk," adds Gumbo. "How are they going to tell our secrets? They cannot say that the British troops are going to Yorktown. Ha! Can you imagine their little mouths trying?"

"Hush up," shushes Tap. "I do not know about any squirrels but there are spies lurking out here. Keep quiet about that stuff."

But it is too late. You have heard their plan. Squirrels may not be able to talk but you sure can!

The End

118

"A moonstruck idea?" you inquire, ignoring your urge to ask General Washington about his teeth.

"James," says George Washington, "can you dance?"

"Excuse me, sir?" you ask.

"If you can dance better than I," says General Washington, "you are the one who will lead my army to independence."

"Is he serious?" you ask, looking at General Lafayette.

"If I were you I would stretch," says Lafayette. "He is quite the dancer."

You cannot believe your ears. The great General George Washington has challenged you to a dance battle! You hand General Lafayette your coat.

Go on to the next page.

"Are you sure you would like to do this, sir?" you ask, touching your toes. General Washington answers your question by pointing at General Lafayette, who promptly begins humming a tune.

General Washington leaps through the air. He gallops about. He steps from side to side. General Lafayette stops humming and General Washington points at you, signaling that it is your turn.

Your future depends on this moment. All you can do is try. You remember how you used to mimic the chickens back on the plantation, making your arms wings and moving about. You click your heels together. Kick your legs up.

"*Oh la la,*" says General Lafayette, joining in on the fun. "That is one funky chicken!"

General Lafayette does it too, laughing beside the two of you. General Washington is overjoyed.

"You are exactly what we need!" he says, clucking and flapping his wings. "A spy should be quick on his feet!"

The End

120

"Pardon me for asking, sir," you say, "but I must inquire about your teeth."

"James," warns General Lafayette.

"He wants to know!" insists General Washington. He turns his back toward the tent. "Stanley!"

"Stanley!" he calls again. "Come here for a moment and bring the family."

A black man leaves one of the tents. He is followed by two children. One is a young boy around four years old and the other is around eight.

You get a bad feeling in your stomach. You meet General Lafayette's eyes, which quickly avert your gaze.

Go on to the next page.

"James," says General Washington. "Meet Stanley. Stanley meet James."

Stanley opens his mouth, revealing a toothless smile. You stumble back in fright. This causes the children to laugh, showing their own snaggle-toothed grins. You stare back at General Washington's mouth in horror. He has filled his mouth with his slave's teeth! You faint, shocked by your discovery...

"How was I to know that the kid can't take a joke?" says General Washington.

"He only joined our barracks yesterday and you have scared him to death," disapproves General Lafayette.

"What can I say?" says General Washington. "I am a very funny man."

"It was a joke?" you repeat.

Turn to the next page.

"Of course," say the two men in unison.

"Then what really happened to your teeth?" you question.

"These lips will never tell," says General Washington. "Every great man needs some sort of mystery, you see."

The End

You do not want to cross the Secret Organization. You tell the generals that you will need to think about their offer before proceeding any further.

Weeks later, you discuss the offer with Sam, John, and Elizabeth when they pay you a visit. The trio agrees to approve your espionage for the Revolutionary Army. They help you maintain your cover along the way. Your shared efforts result in the British Army's defeat at the Battle of Yorktown. This defeat is the first step in the United States of America, becoming its own nation.

When the revolution is over, you remain with the Secret Organization. Although the colonists have won their independence, your people remain in chains. You become an advocate for the voiceless. You work with the group to create a network that offers enslaved people a way to freedom. A century later, a woman named Harriet Tubman will escape slavery and join forces with others to map a system of secret routes between safe houses. The Underground Railroad will bring almost 100,000 enslaved people to freedom.

The End

"I want to see it," you say to Sam, allowing him to show you your future. The child touches a finger to your forehead. You have been transported to a classroom in the twenty-first century.

"This is where children come to learn," says Sam, clapping his hands in delight. "Notice that all sorts of people have the opportunity to sit in these chairs and to receive an education!"

You marvel at the children talking happily as they take their seats. You realize that all the students carry books in their hands. You think that you are mistaken when you see the cover.

"Can it be?" you whisper.

"Chosen," responds Sam, matter-of-factly. "Fated."

You try to pick up a book but fail. Your hand goes through it as if you were grasping at a spiderweb in the wind. Sam carefully grabs the book and hands it to you. Your eyes fill with tears as you turn the book in your palms.

"*James Armistead Lafayette*," you say, reading the cover. "*Spy for the Revolution*."

The End

You follow the drag marks at the edge of the dark cave, and realize with a chill you've made a terrible mistake. This is a wolf den, and you've arrived just in time for dinner. You stand frozen in silence, watching the animals fight over a rabbit carcass. You cannot outrun all of them. The beasts stop eating, realizing that a bigger meal has entered the cave. They turn their bloody snouts toward you. You take the knife out of your pocket, knowing luck is not on your side. You scream as they surround you. It is not long before they begin their feast.

The End

"Alas," you say, taking a step backward. "I think that I will try my luck with John and Elizabeth."

Sam holds up a hand. "You dare to walk away from me?"

"This is all a joke," you say, realizing that your friends must be playing a trick on you. A position in the Revolutionary Army? A secret organization? A magical child? They have truly outdone themselves. They had you going with all the talk of war and victory and independence.

"You doubt my abilities?" asks Sam, his hand closing into a fist. You feel a cool draft caress your neck. If this is a joke, you are finished being the punchline.

"Listen, kid——" you start. Sam interrupts you, offended by your skepticism:

> *If you do not wish to take a look,*
> *your tale of freedom shall be a different book.*
> *If you do not want to see what I do,*
> *there are other ways to make my*
> *predictions true.*

"Hold on," you object, not liking Sam's tone of voice. The child does not seem to hear you. He opens his palm, turning you into a horse. Trapped in this form for the rest of your days, you are ironically renamed Liberty.

The End

ABOUT THE ARTIST

Gabhor Utomo was born in Indonesia. He moved to California to pursue his passion in art. He received his degree from Academy of Art University in San Francisco in spring 2003. Since graduation, he's worked as a freelance illustrator and has illustrated a number of children's books. Gabhor lives with his wife, Dina, and his twin girls in the San Francisco Bay Area.

ABOUT THE AUTHOR

Kyandreia Jones is a Posse Miami Scholar and a Creative Writing major at Hamilton College in Clinton, New York. She was born and raised in South Florida. When she thinks of home she likes to muse that she is in a "sunshine state of mind." Jones' poetry and prose have been published in various college literary publications and magazines such as *Red Weather, Grasping Roots, The Black List Journal,* and *The Underground.* Opportunities like having her first short story "At Home" published by Living Spring Publishers in *Stories Through the Ages, College Edition 2017* inspired Jones to take her writing to new heights. Working for *Choose Your Own Adventure* has been the highlight of Jones' career and she cannot wait to see what other adventures await her! Jones values reading, writing, laughing, and promoting universal kindness.

For games, activities, and other fun stuff, or to write to Kyandreia, visit us online at CYOA.com

The Story of James Armistead Lafayette

James Armistead Lafayette was born in either 1748 or 1760 in Virginia. Good birth records were rare for enslaved persons. He may have been born in New Kent County or Elizabeth City, Virginia. He was considered the property of plantation owner William Armistead until 1781. It was then that James was discovered by the young general Marquis de Lafayette. The Marquis helped James secure permission to leave the plantation and join the side of the colonies in the Revolutionary War.

The war had been raging for six years by 1781. What is now the United States were colonies owned by England, and they were fighting for their freedom to become an independent country. England was separated from the colonies by the Atlantic ocean. The new continent was wild and fierce. Virginia, the colony where James was born and lived, was invaded by the British forces in December 1780. The British generals hoped that doing so would divide the colonies into two: North and South.

The colonists had other problems in 1780: an important colonial general named Benedict Arnold switched sides in the middle of the war. He went from fighting for the colonists to fighting for the British. The first place he went under his new command was to Virginia.

General George Washington, the Commander in Chief, was leading the Revolutionary forces. Washington believed that spying would be critical to beating the British. He believed in it so completely, he was called "America's first spymaster." Washington let the governor of Virginia, Thomas Jefferson, know that Benedict Arnold was invading, but his message was too late and Benedict Arnold burned the city of Richmond to the ground.

When James Armistead signed up for the army in 1781, the colonists in Virginia needed his help. He met General Marquis de Lafayette, a Frenchman who believed slavery was wrong and should be illegal, and agreed to help the colonial army as best he could. Lafayette thought James

Armistead could be something different than a solider: he felt immediately that James would be an excellent spy. And he was right.

James infiltrated the British encampment and convinced Benedict Arnold he was loyal to the English. He formed a network of African Americans who made reports to him that he brought to Lafayette. In May 1781, General Cornwallis arrived in Virginia from England to take over, and Benedict Arnold left the area. James Armistead stayed behind and gained Cornwallis' trust as he had with Arnold. He learned about a planned attack on Yorktown and was able to get the information to George Washington, who was able to surround Cornwallis, forcing a surrender in October, 1781. This effectively ended the war.

Indeed, James Armistead proved to be an extraordinary spy.

Soldiers who had been enslaved were granted their freedom and did not have to return to slavery, but James was considered a spy and not a solider by the new government. He was not granted his freedom when the war ended, despite his incredible contribution. Lafayette was outraged by this decision and helped James petition for his freedom. It took several years, but finally James was granted his freedom in 1787. He took Lafayette's name as his own and received a military pension, which was enough money to afford a farm. He lived on this farm with his wife and family until he reached old age.

Travel was rare during this era, so it took many years for Marquis de Lafayette to return to the United States after the war. In 1824, President James Monroe invited Lafayette to return and tour the new United States. Crowds celebrated Lafayette as a hero everywhere he went. Lafayette traveled to Virginia on his tour and planned to visit George Washington's grave. But before he reached it, he yelled for his carriage to be stopped because he had seen someone he knew in the crowd. He shouted "JAMES!" and the two men rushed through the crowd of gaping people to embrace, two old friends reunited at last.

A History of Slavery and Emancipation in the United States

1619: A Dutch ship, *The White Lion,* brings 20 people who had been captured in their native lands in Africa and enslaved there ashore in Jamestown, Virginia. The colonists are struggling to survive in the wild land. The enslaved African people join indentured Europeans and farm the land.

1662: A Virginia law decreed that the children of enslaved people were also enslaved, for the duration of their lives.

1676: Enslaved African Americans and indentured workers in Virginia joined together in a rebellion against the upper class, crossing racial boundaries with their protest.

1691: Virginia passes a law that makes emancipation of enslaved people expensive and risky, requiring the owner to pay for the newly freed person to leave the colony.

1708: By this date, there were more African Americans in many Southern colonies than people of European origin, and most of the African Americans were enslaved. Plantations became an important part of the economy, growing cotton, tobacco, and rice.

1738: The Seminole tribes of Florida begin to help enslaved African Americans escape there to freedom, and do this for the next 80 years.

1772: A Nigerian man named Ukawfaw Gronniosaw, sold into slavery under accusations of spying, publishes an account of the inhumane conditions of slavery under the pen name James Albert, opening people's eyes to the atrocities being committed on plantations.

1777: Vermont becomes the first state to ban slavery entirely.

1800: A major revolt of enslaved people in Virginia, called Gabriel's Revolt, brings violence and punishment in its wake. It also results in new and much stricter laws.

1821–1822: Liberia is founded as a colony on the continent of Africa, with the intention of creating a place where African Americans fleeing the United States could go.

Around 1831: The Underground Railroad begins with the help of African Americans, Quakers, and others who believe slavery is wrong. Networks of safe houses help bring as many as 100,000 people to freedom over the following decades, but this is still only a small percentage of the people who were enslaved.

1841: A mutiny occurs on the ship *The Amistad*. African people who had been captured and taken aboard to be sold as slaves overtook the ship and were allowed to return to Africa. (1839 captured & 1841 freed.)

1845: Frederick Douglass, a man who escaped slavery, publishes his autobiography, *Narrative of the Life of Frederick Douglass*, which expands his work as an abolitionist of slavery.

1857: In a controversial Supreme Court ruling, the Dred Scott Decision, slavery is upheld as a right by the states.

1859: John Brown, a white abolitionist, leads a raid on Harper's Ferry, Virginia, to protest slavery. He is executed for treason for this act. Many people believe his hanging accelerated the South's secession from the Union.

1860: Abraham Lincoln is elected to a country very divided on the issue of slavery, and seven Southern states secede from the country before he is inaugurated.

1861–1865: The Civil War is fought between the Northern and Southern United States.

1863: The Emancipation Proclamation, signed by Lincoln, officially frees all enslaved people.

1865: Slavery is officially abolished in the U.S. Constitution.

The Culper Code

The cipher used in this book is from the *Culper Code Book,* a real book of codes used during the Revolutionary War by spies who worked for George Washington. George Washington was not only the first President of the United States, he was also noted by many historians to be a big believer in the usefulness of spying.

The Culper Spy Ring was organized in 1778 by Major Benjamin Tallmadge and they created the book together. Each page had numeric codes that matched up with specific words, and sets of letters matched up with other letters. If you had a copy of the book, you could use it to decode secret messages from its 763 different codes.

Spies during the Revolutionary War used the book to create their own spy names, keeping their identities a secret, and also to write coded letters to pass between the generals. It is very likely that James Armistead Lafayette did see and use the *Culper Code Book* during his work as a spy, as he could read and write.